L. Frank Baum's

DOROTHY AND THE WICKED WITCH

Adapted by C. J. Naden
Illustrated by Bill Morrison

Troll Associates

Troll Associates, Mahwah, N.J.

Library of Congress Catalog Card Number: 79-84149
ISBN 0-89375-195-2
ISBN 0-89375-191-X Paper Edition

Dorothy and her little dog Toto stood at the gate of the Emerald City. Behind them waited the Scarecrow, the Tin Woodman, and the Cowardly Lion. They had come to see the Wizard, the wisest of all Wizards. He ruled over this strange Land of Oz. No one had ever seen him. No one knew what he looked like. But Dorothy and her friends had come to ask for his help.

The Wizard's Emerald City was beautiful. But it was strange indeed. Houses and streets and windowpanes sparkled with green. The sky was green. All the people were green. They had green skin and green clothing. And everyone—including Dorothy and her friends, and even Toto—had to wear green glasses. The glasses softened the bright glare of the Emerald City.

"You will be the first to see the great Oz," said a Green
Soldier. He led Dorothy to the Throne Room. What she
saw was a huge chair. On the chair was a huge head. There
was no body, no arms, no legs, no hair. Just one huge head.
"I am the Great and Terrible Oz," said the Head. "What
do you seek?"

"I am the small and meek Dorothy," she said. "A great storm carried my dog Toto and me away from Kansas. We landed in Oz. My house fell on the Wicked Witch of the East and killed her. I am wearing her shoes. The Good Witch of the North kissed my forehead. She told me to come to see you. Only you can get us back to Kansas. I want to go home to Uncle Henry and Aunt Em."

"If you wish me to help you," said the Great Head of Oz, "you must help me first. You must get rid of the Wicked Witch of the West." Dorothy shook her head. "But I can't," she cried.

"You destroyed the Wicked Witch of the East, and now you are wearing her shoes. There is only one Wicked Witch left in Oz. Get rid of her," said the Wizard, "and I will send you home to Kansas."

The Scarecrow was next in the Throne Room. This time the Wizard looked like a lovely lady. "I am only a scarecrow," said the Scarecrow. "My head is stuffed with straw. I know that you can give me brains. I need them badly." The Lovely Lady of Oz replied, "Destroy the Wicked Witch of the West. Then I will give you brains."

Then the Tin Woodman went into the Throne Room.
Now the Wizard looked like a hideous beast as large as an
elephant. Luckily for the Woodman, he was not afraid. "I
have come to ask for a heart," he said. "Then I will be like
everyone else." The Beast replied, "Destroy the Wicked
Witch of the West. Then I will give you a heart."

The Cowardly Lion went to the Throne Room. All he saw was a great ball of fire. "I am cowardly," said the Lion. "I am afraid of everything. I want some courage so that I may be King of the Beasts." The Ball of Fire said, "Destroy the Wicked Witch of the West. Then I will give you courage."

"The Wicked Witch of the West lives in the Land of the Winkies," Dorothy said to her friends. "How can we get rid of her? Oh dear, Toto and I will never get back to Kansas." The Scarecrow said, "And I will never have brains." The Tin Woodman moaned, "And I will never have a heart." The Cowardly Lion sobbed, "And I will never feel courage."

"But I suppose we must try," said Dorothy. And everyone agreed. They went to the Gatekeeper of the Emerald City. "Where is the road to the Wicked Witch of the West?" asked Dorothy. "There is no road," said the Gatekeeper. "No one ever wants to go there." Dorothy sighed. "Then how can we find her?" she said.

"Oh, that's easy," said the Gatekeeper. "As soon as you are there, the Witch will find *you*—and make you her slaves." The friends began walking to the West. Soon the Emerald City was far behind them. But there was no road, and the ground was rough. Dorothy and Toto and the Lion lay down to sleep. The Scarecrow and the Woodman stood guard. They were never sleepy.

Far away, the Wicked Witch of the West was looking out of the castle window. The Witch had only one eye, but it was very powerful. She could see everywhere. She saw Dorothy and the Lion and Toto asleep. Quickly, the Witch blew her silver whistle. At once a great band of shaggy wolves appeared.

"Tear them to pieces!" shouted the Wicked Witch. But the Scarecrow and the Woodman saw the wolves coming. The Woodman woke everyone and shouted, "Get behind me!" So fast did the Woodman swing his axe that all forty wolves soon lay dead. The Wicked Witch was very angry to see a pile of dead wolves.

The Witch blew her silver whistle once again. This time a great flock of wild crows flew out. When the Scarecrow saw them, he shouted to the others. "Lie down beside me!" Crows are always afraid of scarecrows. Then the Scarecrow twisted the neck of each and every one. Needless to say, the Wicked Witch was very angry to see a pile of dead crows.

Next, the Wicked Witch sent some Winkies to capture the little group. The Winkies were her slaves. They had to obey her. But the Lion roared fearfully and frightened them away. So the Witch used her magic Golden Cap. She called the Winged Monkeys to come to her. She had already used the cap twice before. This would be the last time the Winged Monkeys would ever have to obey her.

"Destroy them!" shouted the Wicked Witch. "But bring the Lion to me. I will put the huge beast to work." The Winged Monkeys dropped the Tin Woodman on a pile of rocks. He was so dented that he could not move. They pulled all the straw out of the Scarecrow. He was so limp that he could not move. They tied up the Lion and flew him to the castle.

But the Winged Monkeys could not hurt Dorothy. They
saw the mark on her forehead where she had been kissed
by the Good Witch of the North. So, instead, they carried
Dorothy and Toto to the castle. The Wicked Witch could
not hurt Dorothy either. "But I can make you my slave,"
she said. "And I will get those magic shoes you wear," she
thought to herself.

19

Dorothy did not know the shoes were magic. But she never took them off, except at night when she went to bed. The Wicked Witch was afraid of the dark. *How would she get the shoes?* In the meantime, she made Dorothy her slave. And poor Dorothy had to work from dawn to dusk. She was very sad. Now she would never get home to Kansas.

Then one day Dorothy tripped on the castle floor. One of her silver shoes fell off. Quick as a wink, the Wicked Witch snatched it up. Dorothy was very angry. "You are a wicked creature," she cried. Then she picked up a bucket of water and splashed the water all over the Wicked Witch of the West.

"Oh, horrors!" screamed the Witch. "Water means the end of me. I shall melt away." Before Dorothy's astonished eyes, the Wicked Witch melted into a big puddle. Dorothy put on her silver shoes. Then she swept the puddle right out the castle door. The Wicked Witch was dead.

How happy the Winkies were! At last they were free. Dorothy ran to unlock the Lion's cage. Now he was free, too. "If only we could find our friends the Scarecrow and the Tin Woodman," said the Cowardly Lion. "Then I would be happy."

"We can find them for you," said the Winkies. They were so glad to be free that they wanted to help. Soon the little Winkies, who were always dressed in yellow, scattered over the land. They found the Tin Woodman. He was battered and bent and rusty. He could not move at all. But the Winkies carried him back to the castle.

"Do you have some tinsmiths?" Dorothy asked the Winkies when she saw the poor Woodman. Indeed they did. And the tinsmiths went right to work. They pounded and polished and straightened and oiled. When they were done, the Tin Woodman had some patches here and there. But he was just as good as new.

"But where is the Scarecrow?" sobbed the Cowardly Lion. Once more the yellow Winkies scattered across the land. They found the poor limp Scarecrow and carried him to the castle. The Winkies stuffed the Scarecrow with clean fresh straw. And behold! The Scarecrow was as good as new.

Dorothy and her friends spent a few happy days with the Winkies. But at last she said, "We must go back to the Emerald City. The Wizard has promised to send Toto and me home to Uncle Henry and Aunt Em in Kansas. I love you all, but I do want to go home." The Scarecrow nodded. "And I want some brains," he said. "A heart," said the Woodman. "And courage," said the Cowardly Lion.

Before they left, Dorothy put on the Wicked Witch's Golden Cap. She did not know it was magic. Then off they went to the Emerald City. But the Land of the Winkies had no roads. So they were soon lost. Dorothy bent her head in sadness. And when she did, the Golden Cap fell off.

"Oh, look!" cried Dorothy. "There are words written on the lining." And she read them aloud. Then, right before their eyes, a band of Winged Monkeys appeared. "What is your command?" asked the King Monkey. "We wish to go to the Emerald City," said Dorothy.

Before they knew what was happening, the Monkeys picked them all up and carried them high into the air. Soon they saw the Emerald City shining below. The Monkeys set them carefully on the ground and flew away. "Thank you and goodbye," Dorothy called.

"You're back!" said the Gatekeeper in great surprise. "I thought you were going to see the Wicked Witch of the West." The Scarecrow said, "We did, but she is melted." The Gatekeeper was even more surprised. "That is good news indeed," he said. "I suppose you want to see the Wizard right away." He gave them the green glasses and led them once more to the Wizard's castle.

"Now the Wizard will get me back to Kansas," said Dorothy. "I'll have brains," said the Scarecrow with a wise smile. "Oz will give me a heart," said the Woodman with his hand over his chest. "And at last I will have courage," roared the Cowardly Lion. But Toto, who was trotting along behind, just gave a loud bark.